Carly's Stories

by Ken Ainsworth
illustrated by Ruth Ohi

Annick Press Ltd.
Toronto • New York

Lindsey loves her little sister.

Yesterday Carly came up to her and said, “D’you know what? D’you know what? I saw a baby bore.” Carly is always telling stories.

Lindsey said, "Really? You saw a bear? Where did you see it?"

"I saw the bore walking in the middle of the steet, but not on the highway. And d'you know what? That baby bore did see a lion and a tiger. And that baby bore did see a water place, and it was empty. And that mommy and daddy bore

did see that baby in the swimming pool; they did go in and did lift the baby bore out."

Sometimes Lindsey gets confused by parts of Carly's stories. She asked, "How did that baby bear get into the swimming pool?"

"That bore did jump in to get the ball. It was a pink ball."

appy
birthday

"Oh, I thought maybe the baby bear was scared of the lion and the tiger."

"Nope. Cause d'you know what? They were babies too, and dat baby bore did go and play with them."

"Oh, I see. That was a good story, Carly. Do you want to play baby bear now?"

"Okay," said Carly with a big smile.

They pretended that Carly was a baby bear and Lindsey was a little girl who found her. Lindsey gave her some food. Then she wrapped her in blankets and put her to bed.

But that baby bear was restless. She kept getting up again. She also chewed on Lindsey's teddy bear and scared one of the babies. Lindsey was glad when it was time to stop playing and go to bed.

This morning, when Lindsey woke up, she picked a book and went and found Daddy so they could have their morning cuddle. They were sitting in the big green chair when Carly came out of her room. She was all sleepy and cosy-looking in her fluffy pink sleeper.

She said, with a very serious look on her face, "Daddy, why did you shoot that tain?"

Daddy looked surprised. "I was shooting a train?"

"Yup," said Carly.

Daddy smiled. "I think it was a dream, honey."

"Nope, it wasn't," said Carly. "Why were you shooting it?"

"Well, um, were you scared of it? Was it trying to hurt you?"

"Yup, I was scared of it." Carly had an even more serious look on her chubby face.

Lindsey covered her smile with her hand and peeked at Daddy. He asked Carly what the train had looked like.

"D'you know what? The head was black and the back was another colour. Daddy? Did that tain have eyes?"

"Well, um," Daddy said, "trains don't have eyes. They have people who drive them."

Lindsey went and found a book with a picture of a train and showed Carly.

Carly said, "Nope, it didn't look like that."

"Have you ever seen one before?" Daddy asked.

"Yup," said Carly, nodding her head quickly. "Remember that tain you shooted?"

Daddy and Lindsey felt like smiling really hard at Carly's story, but they didn't let her know.

Daddy gave Carly a hug so she wouldn't feel sad any more and said, "Well, Daddy was probably trying to stop that train from hurting you."

"Yup," she said, nodding her head. "Daddy, d'you know what? Teddy said that a bad tain did take Mommy away. Daddy? When is Mommy coming home?"

Daddy wrapped his arms around both of the girls and said, "Mommy is going to be home today, Carly, after lunch-time, remember? She just went to stay with Grandma and Grandpa when Grandpa was sick."

"Ooh," said Carly, "after lunch-time! Today?"

"Yes," said Daddy, "today. Why don't you and Lindsey go out and pick some flowers to put on the table for Mommy?"

"Okay," said Carly. Then she frowned again. "Daddy, are youse going to make lunch?"

"Well, yes, I am."

"Yorse lunches are yucky," said Carly seriously, and Daddy started laughing.

"Well, today I'll try making your sandwich the way Mommy does," he said.

stop
go

After breakfast Carly and Lindsey went out and picked dandelions for the table. Then they played going for a trip on a nice train. Lindsey doesn't want Carly to be scared.

She loves her little sister.

And Carly loves Lindsey back.

Cover design: Sheryl Shapiro

Annick Press Ltd.

Annick Press gratefully acknowledges the support of the Canada Council and the Ontario Arts Council.

Canadian Cataloguing in Publication Data

Ainsworth, Ken, 1957-
Carly's stories

ISBN 1-55037-381-1 (bound) ISBN 1-55037-380-3 (pbk.)

I. Ohi, Ruth. II. Title.

PS8550.I67C37 1994 jC813'.54 C94-932299-7
PZ7.A55Ca 1994

The art in this book was rendered in watercolours.
The text was typeset in Futura by Attic Typesetting.

Distributed in Canada by:
Firefly Books Ltd.
250 Sparks Ave.
Willowdale, ON M2H 2S4

Published in the U.S.A. by Annick Press (U.S.) Ltd.
Distributed in the U.S.A. by:
Firefly Books (U.S.) Inc.
P.O. Box 1338
Ellicott Station
Buffalo, NY 14205

Printed on acid-free paper.

Printed and bound in Canada by
D.W. Friesen & Sons, Altona, Manitoba.